EARTHLETS
as explained by
Professor Xargle

Library of Congress Cataloging-in-Publication Data
Willis, Jeanne.
    Earthlets, as explained by Professor Xargle/by Jeanne Willis;
illustrated by Tony Ross.—1st American ed.
        p.   cm.
        Originally published: London: Andersen Press, 1988.
        Summary: Professor Xargle's class of extraterrestrials learns
about the physical characteristics and behavior of the human baby.
        ISBN 0-525-44465-3
        [1. Extraterrestrials—Fiction.   2. Babies—Fiction.] I. Ross,
Tony. ill.   II. Title.
PZ7.W68313Ear   1989   88-23692
[E]—dc19   CIP
                                                                 AC

First published in the United States in 1989
by Dutton Children's Books,
a division of Penguin Books USA Inc.
375 Hudson Street, New York, New York 10014
Originally published in Great Britain in 1988
by Andersen Press Ltd.,
20 Vauxhall Bridge Road, London SW1

Printed in Hong Kong
8   10   9   7

EARTHLETS
as explained by
Professor Xargle

by Jeanne Willis
illustrated by Tony Ross

DUTTON CHILDREN'S BOOKS   NEW YORK

Good morning, class.

Today we are going to learn about Earthlets.

Earthlets come in different colors: pink, brown, black and yellow, but not green.

They have one head but only two eyes. And they have two short tentacles and two longer ones, with feelers on the ends.

They use their feelers to help them catch wild animals called Fluffy and Kitty.

Earthlets grow fur on their heads, but not enough to keep them warm.

So they are wrapped in the fuzz of sheep.

Earthlings called Grandmas unravel the fuzz.
Then with two pointed sticks, they make it into
Earthlet wrappers.

Earthlets are born without fangs. At first, they drink only milk, through a hole in their faces called a mouth.

When they finish the milk, they are patted and squeezed so they won't explode.

After an Earthlet grows fangs, the parent Earthling
sometimes takes a banana or the egg of a hen and
mashes it with a shiny tool.

The mash is put on a little shovel and tipped into the
Earthlet's mouth, nose and ears.

Earthlets often leak. When they do, their bottom
tentacles are raised so the Earthlet can be pinned
into a white cloth or sealed in soft paper with tape.

During the day, Earthlets collect dirt, Fluffy hair, milk, and banana-mash.

Then they are placed in a plastic capsule with warm water and a floating bird.

After soaking, they must be dried carefully so they won't shrink. Then they are sprinkled with dust so they won't stick to things.

An Earthlet can be recognized by its roar:
"WAAAAAAAH!"

To quiet the Earthlet, the father Earthling flings it into the atmosphere.

But he never ever drops it.

If the Earthlet keeps roaring, its mother pulls its feelers and says "This little piggy went to market" until the Earthlet makes *hee hee* noises.

At night the Earthlet goes to a place called beddy-bye.

This is a rocking box that is soft inside. A small bear called Teddy lives there.

That is the end of today's lesson.

Now let's all put on our disguises and go see some real Earthlets.

The spaceship leaves for planet Earth in five minutes.